LEARNING ABC
AND MORALITY

LEARNING ABC AND MORALITY

LAMA ANI PELMA

LEARNING ABC AND MORALITY

iUniverse books may be ordered through booksellers or by contacting:

iUniverse
1663 Liberty Drive
Bloomington, IN 47403
www.iuniverse.com
844-349-9409

ISBN: 978-1-6632-1417-1 (sc)
ISBN: 978-1-6632-1418-8 (e)

Print information available on the last page.

iUniverse rev. date: 01/23/2021

Dedication

This book is dedicated to Marie
Placide (book illustrator's mom)

Evia Placide RIP 1994

It is interesting how we miss others more after their
death. She was loving, considerate and kind. She
was a dedicated wife that kept the family vibrant.

Introduction

We would like all the children of the universe to learn some basic moral principles and values while they are having fun coloring with their friends.

When I was growing up, I did not have the opportunity of incorporating art as a medium for education. It was always used to entertain us.

This book is one of the many ways of reaching all of the children of the universe to teach more about ethics and morality.

Contents

Acknowledgements

Special thanks to:

Veronica & Michael
Denis Clarke
Venerable Marie Placide
Bowie community and missionaries
my sponsors
teachers
Carolyn Massey
Floss Barber
Betty Sager
Dr. Word Smith
Susan Brannan
Elianna Morris
And all the special angels that protect me.

A

Angels can guide
you through your life
every day, if you pray
and believe
in them.

B

Bells usually make beautiful noises. They are also used in churches and temples for special events.

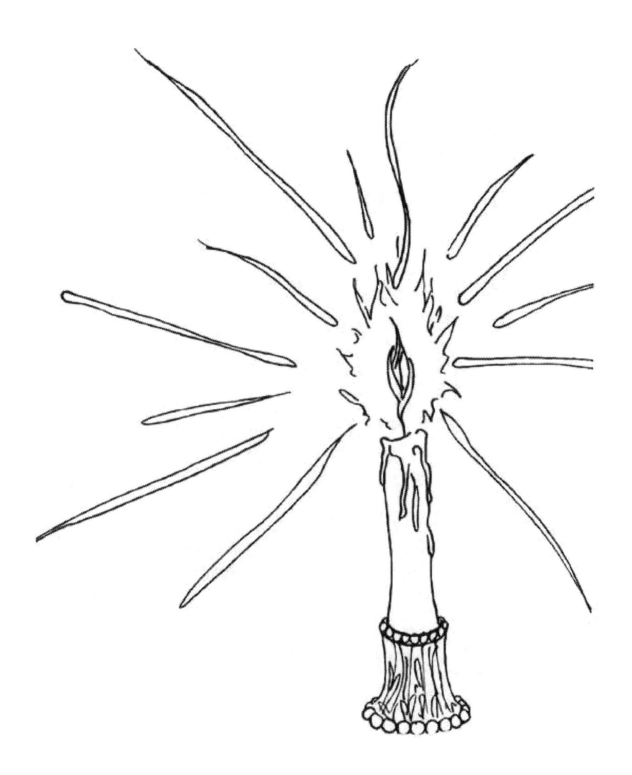

C

Candles bring a special light to all the children of the universe

Dear friends at school are good to have but you must treat them the way you want to be treated.

E

Evil is doing
and saying bad
things to someone
you know.

F

You should have *Faith* when you pray so that your prayers will get answered.

G

Doing *good* will bring you good things.

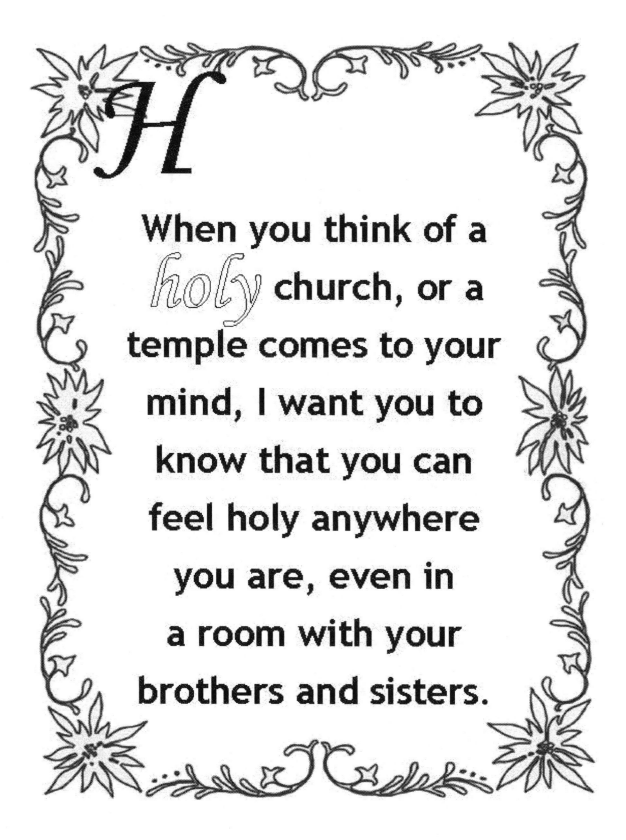

H

When you think of a *holy* church, or a temple comes to your mind, I want you to know that you can feel holy anywhere you are, even in a room with your brothers and sisters.

17

I

Most of the time you think you are hiding your *inner* feelings like anger, but your mommy can see it expressed in your beautiful face.

J

There is a special *joy*
that comes from giving
and sharing your things
with other kids.

K

Once upon a time, there was a *King* in a great big castle. He was a fair ruler. He treated rich kids and poor kids the same way. He had no favourites. You might not be a king, but you can treat all the children of the universe the same.

L

Don't give mommy and daddy a kiss because you want to go and play at your friend's house or because you want a new toy; just *love* both of them all the time without a reason.

Money can be
used for good and bad
reasons. You can use it
to buy grandma a gift
or you can use it to buy
something to play a prank
on your friend at school.
You should always use it
for buying good things
or doing good things or
doing good deeds.

N

You should love the kid in the class who everyone thinks is a genius, even though his drawing looks better than yours. You should love him like your *neighbour.*

O

Although we daydream about living in a big house, driving in a sports car and having all the designer clothing, these things are *outer* and material. You should learn to be kind, sweet and gentle. These things can be great inner qualities.

At home and school, you should *pray* and thank your special Angel for your meal and health and family. You should not pray only when you need something but also to thank your special Angel for His goodness, help and love.

Q

It is always nice to have *quiet* time where you can reflect on your day and think how you can become a better boy or girl.

R

The *rays* of sunshine will always warm your heart, so you must also learn to warm grandpa's heart by giving him big, big, hugs.

S

Your *soul* is like a very precious gem, so you should cherish it with good thoughts and actions. This will make you shine like a gem.

T

Speaking the *truth* is always the best thing to do, even when it hurts your feelings to do so. If you took cookies without permission from your mommy and she asked you, please be honest and tell the whole truth. Do not lie.

U

There are many different children in the *universe.* They all have different cultures and lifestyles. We should not judge them because we do not speak the same language. Or because we do not understand them.

V

It is not a good thing for a little boy or girl to be *vain*. We should not worship things because we are going to leave them on earth when we die.

W There are many forms of *worship.* In the United States, most people worship Jesus and in the eastern countries prayers are recited to the Buddha. These are just two of the many religions in the world.

X

Tic tac toe is a good game to play with X and O. When we play games we should follow all the rules and not cheat at all.

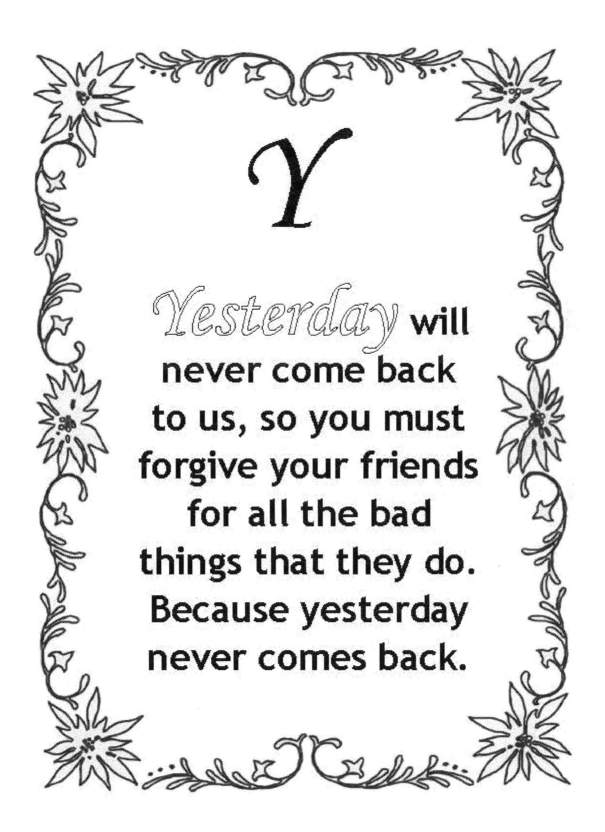

Y

Yesterday will never come back to us, so you must forgive your friends for all the bad things that they do. Because yesterday never comes back.

Zebras have black and white stripes and they are fun to look at. Sometimes in life your friends may be born into different cultures and we should be kind to all of them because they are also beautiful children of the universe, just like you.

About the Author

Lama Ani Pelma was born in Barbados. She completed two three-year retreats in the desert. Living simply and meditating are some of the key factors in her lifestyle; not to mention trying to stay on a journey of keeping her moral code as a nun for 27 years. The journey remains mesmerizing for her. There is never a dull moment. Praying with great faith is one of her favorite past times.

She is working on a poetry book at the same time as Learning ABC & Morality. Windows Of My Dream which is captivating, lusty, deep, and spiritual. May these books enhance your daily practices.

She and her class at DMU authored The Ultimate Offering in 2009. It is a ritual text about how to make offerings.